Dulk

I Had This Dream

K.G. Radford

AuthorHouse™ UK
1663 Liberty Drive
Bloomington, IN 47403 USA
www.authorhouse.co.uk
Phone: 0800.197.4150

Published by AuthorHouse 11/22/2017

ISBN: 978-1-5462-8493-2 (sc)
ISBN: 978-1-5462-8511- 3 (e)

Library of Congress Control Number: 2017917674

Print information available on the last page.

This book is printed on acid-free paper.

authorHOUSE®

ACKNOWLEDGMENT

*I would like to dedicate my first book **"Dulk"** to my lovely wife, my beautiful daughters and to my grandchildren.*

They are my inspiration to publish this book.

Thank you to my team consultants from Author House UK for all your support!

Dulk had a problem getting to sleep. Not only did his cat, called Sulk, take most of the bed, but he kept dreaming, dreaming and dreaming.

The next morning, Dulk jumped out of the bed, got dressed and raced to the kitchen for his breakfast.

He could not get enough breakfast bricks into his bowl. Greedy Dulk!

He had his usual three bowls full and then made a cup of tea.

'I'd love a nice cuppa green tea.
   Only a small one,' he thought. 'Ah....! that's better!'

When he had finished his cuppa, he thought he would have a wander into his special garden.
   Maybe, just maybe, the plants and animals might speak with him. You never know, sometimes dreams come true.

'Now, where did I put my gardening clothes, my gardening hat and gardening boots?' he thought.

Dulk was very proud of his giant mushrooms. 'I'll try to speak to them,' he thought.

'Hello!' he said, 'bet there's not much room in there?' he jokingly asked.

And to his surprise....

He heard a very soft voice.

'Hellooo! Mr. Dulk! Thank you for growing us and looking after us,' said the largest and tallest mushroom.

Dulk didn't know what to do or say, or say or do.

'Am I hearing things?' he said to himself.

'No! No! No! You are not!' replied the mushrooms in order of size.

'How did you know my name?' asked Dulk.

'All of the other plants and animals told us,' replied the largest mushroom.

'You mean that you all can talk to each other?' enquired Dulk.

'That's right,' replied the middle size mushroom.

'Why haven't you spoke to me before?' sighed Dulk.
    'Because you always look sad and angry,' squeaked the smallest flower.

'Oh, dear!' groaned Dulk, 'I'd better change the looks on my face then.'
    I'll ask some of the vegetables, fruits and flowers.
    'Will they talk to me if I keep a smile on my face?' he asked.

'Oh! Yes! Of course!' they all replied.
    'Yippee! Cool! Mr. Dulk you are smiling and look very happy and friendly,' shouted the flowers and weeping onion.

Happy Dulk!

Dulk woke up in bed and sat up.

He was smiling.

'I wonder if I was really dreaming?' he pondered.

Dulk jumped out of bed, got dressed and raced to the kitchen for his brick breakfast.

He could not get enough breakfast bricks into his bowl.
Very greedy Dulk!

He had his usual three bowls full and then made a cup of green tea.

When he had finished his tea, he thought he would visit his special garden.

'I wonder if the plants, vegetables and flowers do actually talk?' he said.

'This is all getting very exciting and interesting,' he giggled.

So, he went to change into his gardening clothes.

He was so curious and excited, that he forgot to put on his hat and ran as fast as he could, into his special garden.

He found a large plant pot to sit on and smiled at his secret giant peas.

'These, are why my garden is so special and magical,' he whispered.

'If I speak with them now, I wonder if they will speak back to me, then my dream will have come true!' he thought.

'Hello giant peas!' he shouted.

All of the peas opened their eyes and gave beautiful wide smiles.

'Hello, hello, hello, hello, hello, hello, hello, hello, hello, hello, hello, hello, and hello!' they all replied.

'Thank you for speaking to us,' they giggled.

'My magic plant food has obviously worked!' he said to himself.

'Did you all enjoy growing inside your pea pods?' he asked.

'Yes!' they replied, 'plenty of good plant food, water, sunshine and we kept each other nice and warm by hugging together.'

'Oh! Good! Are you all tasty giant sweet peas?' Dulk asked jokingly.

'Of course!' was the happy answer.

Dulk put the peas down and walked back through his special garden.

He felt so proud of his achievements, being able to speak with the plants and growing large vegetation.

'I must keep my secrets to myself,' he said, 'you must not tell anyone! I need a nice cuppa,' he sighed.

'Maybe, I might have another dream in bed tonight and who knows.....it might come true!' he smiled.

'Let us see what tomorrow brings,' thought Dulk. 'Wow!'

'I wonder if I can put my dreams to any good? Conversing with the plants and using my special plant food! Cool Dulk!

Bring on another dream!' yelled Dulk.

CPSIA information can be obtained at www.ICGtesting.com
Printed in the USA
LVIW01n0059040118
561733LV00004B/26